Samantha Alexander lives in Lincolnshire with a variety of animals including her thoroughbred horse, Bunny, and her two kittens, Cedric and Bramble. Her schedule is almost as busy and exciting as her plots – she writes a number of columns for newspapers and magazines, is a teenage agony aunt for BBC Radio Leeds and in her spare time she regularly competes in dressage and showjumping.

Books by Samantha Alexander available from Macmillan

RIDING SCHOOL

HOLLYWELL STABLES

RIDING SCHOOL

4
Kate

SAMANTHA ALEXANDER

MACMILLAN CHILDREN'S BOOKS

First published 1999 by Macmillan Children's Books
a division of Macmillan Publishers Ltd
25 Eccleston Place, London SW1W 9NF
Basingstoke and Oxford
www.macmillan.co.uk
Associated companies throughout the world

ISBN 0 330 36839 7

3 5 7 9 8 6 4

A CIP catalogue record for this book is available from
the British Library.

Phototypeset by Intype London Limited
Printed and bound in Great Britain by
Mackays of Chatham plc, Chatham, Kent

*Samantha Alexander and
Macmillan Children's Books would like
to thank all at Suzanne's Riding School,
especially Suzanne Marczak.*

Chapter One

"There's no such thing as ghosts," I said emphatically, staring at Emma who really believed in the stable phantom.

Somebody had been spreading rumours that Brook House Riding School was haunted. Of course the whole idea was ridiculous.

"Oh yeah, so why are the lessons only half full? And why does nobody want to stay after dark? Even Jodie won't go in the barn by herself," said Emma.

"That's a lie." Jodie suddenly perked up after staring mindlessly through the saloon window for fifteen minutes. "I don't mind ghosts – in fact I feel quite sorry for them. They're tragic figures from the past just trying to put things right."

I groaned out loud.

Rachel and Steph sat on the table swinging their legs, their eyes wide with fear. Rachel was so stewed up about imaginary hoof beats and mysterious cigar smoke she wouldn't go to the toilet without someone outside standing guard.

"I don't believe you lot," I said, exasperated. "Someone invents a Christmas hoax like this and you all fall for it hook, line and sinker." It was twelve days before Christmas and instead of a partridge in a pear tree we had a resident poltergeist.

"OK Kate, Miss Know-it-all, if you're so brave, why don't you stay here by yourself this afternoon, when we go out for a ride?" said Steph.

Sophie, who'd been making Christmas crackers with horsy treats in the centre – one for each riding school pony – suddenly joined in. "It's a Six Pack dare."

The Six Pack was our own special club – Jodie, Sophie, Rachel, Emma, Steph and myself. To join you had to be horse-crazy and dedicated to helping out with the riding school ponies. We even had membership badges which had been donated by a famous horse trainer, Josh le Fleur. I instinctively touched mine, pinned on my shirt under three jumpers.

"Piece of cake," I answered glibly, seeing the perfect solution. "I'm going to prove to each one of you, once and for all that there really are no such things as ghosts."

I didn't know at that time that I was going to be scared out of my wits. I really had no idea.

*

"See you later. Don't let the bugs bite – or rather ghosts," Steph tittered. Then she pulled her coat over her head and made a hooting noise which sounded more like an owl with a sore throat than a banshee.

Sophie rode up on Rocket adjusting her stirrups followed by Emma on Buzby and Rachel on Rusty. "Are you sure this is what you want?" Sophie's voice was loaded with concern.

I rolled my eyes and looked heavenwards. "Do I really need to answer that one more time?"

"You can put some of Monty's garlic supplement in your pockets if you want," Steph generously offered. "Garlic's supposed to ward off evil." Her mouth twitched mischievously.

Nine ponies and four horses clattered reluctantly out of the yard in single file, nose to tail. Five members of the Six Pack followed on behind. Sandra, the full-time groom, led the ride on Frank, a part Shire with soup-plate feet and the acceleration of a steam engine.

"We probably won't be back until midnight at this rate," Steph grumbled, tucking in behind Rocket.

"Don't say that." Emma's baby blue eyes widened in horror. She said in a whisper, "What if the ghost follows us? He could do – it's perfectly possible."

3

"I think you've been watching too many *X-Files*," Sophie tutted.

"Don't worry, Em," I said lightly. "I'll hobble the horses and hide your skateboard. That should pin him down for a while."

Emma pursed her lips into a thin, wounded line. "The trouble with you, Kate," she said in a tight voice, "is that you know absolutely nothing about the supernatural."

It started to get misty. I shuddered with cold and went to get my jacket from the saloon. The riding school was deserted.

Guy, the instructor, had gone to stock up with horse food. Tuesday afternoons were always quiet – there was only a ride today because it was the Christmas holidays. Revelling in the peace and quiet, I fantasized about running the yard myself. I was a famous dressage rider in sole charge of a string of mega-expensive horses. People paid me fortunes just to sit on their horses. It was expected that I'd pick up the gold medal at the next Olympics.

I scanned the stables critically, through the eyes of a champion. No loose straw, no pitchforks out of place, everything immaculate. I nodded with approval. I must thank my grooms. But first I'd check on my top horse, Archie. Dear, wonderful

Archie. He was now world-famous, renowned for being difficult but brilliant with the best piaffe the world had ever seen.

"Archie?" I shouted his name.

After a five-second delay he appeared over the door, trailing hay and sporting a brown and green stable stain over his right ear and eye. As a creamy Palomino, Archie's favourite pastime was getting as dirty as possible. He now resembled some kind of equine pirate. I scratched his nose which he loved and pushed his thatch of mane onto the right side.

What was that? My spine tingled with alarm. I was convinced I'd seen something out of the corner of my eye – a shadow, a shape, a body. I tried to ignore the horrid lurching sensation in my stomach. It couldn't be . . . It wasn't . . . I forced myself to look up and then swooned with relief. It was a black bin bag caught on the fence. How could I have been so stupid? I was furious with myself for listening to Emma's ridiculous stories. Still weak with relief, I started to sing "Oh Come All Ye Faithful" and stomped across to the tack room.

I tried not to pay too much attention to Archie who was suddenly tense, his eyes fixed on the barn, every nerve strained taut.

The tap was turned on. Full blast. Drat. Somebody must have forgotten. Water spurted all over, seeping under the stable doors.

I turned it off quickly and climbed the stone steps to the tack room, contemplating cleaning Archie's tack. Inside, I ripped open a packet of crisps and put my feet up on the saddle horse. Then I froze. Straight in front of me was a row of bridles which were usually all hung neatly under different nameplates. Nothing odd about that. Only something had happened. They were all turned round, back to front, upside down, jostled around. Two were even strewn on the floor.

Normally, I would have sworn some of the younger kids had been messing about but I knew that I had been the last one in there and that was barely fifteen minutes earlier.

Fear rose in my throat. I could feel my heart beginning to accelerate. Then the tap started running outside. Somebody had turned it back on. Slowly, I backed out of the tack room. I could barely breathe.

I was terrified. I tried to take deep breaths and closed my eyes briefly, but it was no good. Everywhere eyes seemed to be boring into me, watching, waiting, laughing.

I could hear water rushing over the concrete. Not even daring to look, I bolted for the saloon and slammed the door. Here, at least, I felt safe.

6

Here, where we had lunch, hung out, read magazines, told jokes. I could almost hear the other girls laughing. I had to get a grip and calm down.

I took a deep breath and my stomach lurched with hot terror. The whole room stank of cigar smoke. Sickly, fresh, scouring my nostrils. I whimpered hysterically and backed into a corner, my knees buckling as I slid down the wall. Tears streaked my face. I covered my ears with my hands, blocking out the roaring water. I snapped my eyes shut and buried my head in my knees. I repeated poems over and over that we'd learnt in English and then silly snippets of songs and endless nursery rhymes. My legs prickled with pins and needles. I was aching cold but I didn't move. I didn't dare.

"Kate, whatever is it, what's the matter?" Suddenly Sophie's arms were around me, pulling me to my feet. Jodie and Emma were with her.

"Can you smell it?" I trembled, my eyes bright with tears.

"Kate, what are you talking about?" Sophie stared into my face, trying to read my thoughts. "I can't smell a thing."

"Here, drink this, it'll make you feel better." Emma passed me a plastic cup of tea and half a Kit Kat. "Chocolate's good for shock."

"According to you chocolate's good for everything," I mumbled, trying to make a stab at humour but really feeling sick with relief that it was all over. I felt washed out, drained, exhausted. I sipped at the tea and burnt my tongue.

"So you really saw the ghost?" Emma stared, white-faced but obviously impressed.

"Um, well, not quite." Somehow I didn't like to spoil the moment by telling the exact truth.

"You're so brave," said Rachel, full of awe. "I'd have died on the spot."

"What did it look like?" Emma's imagination was working overtime. "Did it float or walk? Did it say anything? Was it a man or a woman?"

Fresh horror made me choke on the tea. "Er, I kind of didn't hang around to find out. Like I said, it sort of chased me in here."

Rachel oozed admiration. I could see a heavy bout of hero worship coming on.

"Serves you right for not believing in ghosts in the first place," Steph grumbled, clearly annoyed that she hadn't seen it first.

"I don't think we should be talking about it here," mouthed Sophie. "We might hurt its feelings. It's obviously very distressed about something."

"Sophie, this isn't a Steven Spielberg movie. I'm sure it's not hovering above us listening in to every word." Jodie rolled her eyes contemptuously. "You really do have a poor understanding of the spirit world."

"And I suppose you've written a book on it," Sophie threw back with irritation. Jodie always behaved like she was twelve going on twenty.

"Maybe we should just forget all about it," I said with a grimace. "I'm really not feeling up to all this." All I wanted to do was go home and lie in a hot bath listening to Boys One.

"We haven't decided what we're going to do." Jodie pursed her lips, flicking her blond hair behind her ears.

"I hadn't realized this was a Six Pack meeting," I groaned, sitting back down heavily.

"Well, before it was all a kind of joke," said Jodie, clasping her hands together. "I have to admit, I did kind of make up a couple of things to get everyone going, just for a laugh."

Sophie looked outraged.

"Actually me too." Steph grinned sheepishly. "I didn't really see a strange woman dressed as a nun."

"Steph, how could you?" Emma looked mortally wounded. "I really believed you."

"The thing is," Jodie went on, taking charge as usual, "should we tell anyone what Kate's experienced?"

Despite my headache I felt suddenly deflated at

9

the prospect of not being able to boast just a little bit.

"What we've got to decide is . . ." Jodie paused for dramatic effect, "will anyone really want to come to a riding school that's haunted?"

Chapter Two

"Well, it's obvious what's happened, isn't it?" Emma pulled on a pair of luminous yellow mittens which she swore were riding gloves. "The ghost's done a bunk. It's taken one look at Kate and skedaddled. Decided it was out of its league."

I glared at Emma but decided not to rise to the bait. Nothing strange had happened for four days. It was almost an anticlimax. I was beginning to really believe I'd dreamt the whole thing.

"It says here that some people are more tuned in to spirits than others, and that ghosts can take many forms and are usually linked to a tragic happening from the past," said Steph.

"I could have told you that," Jodie tutted.

Steph had borrowed *101 Fascinating Facts About Ghosts* from the library. "Did you know that quartz crystals ward off evil spirits?"

"Oh great, I'll just pop down to the supermarket then and order some," I said.

"Oh, be serious." Steph pulled a face. "It says

11

here that spirits usually appear when some change has been made to their environment."

"Well, that's it then. Guy moved the muck heap, remember? It obviously couldn't stand the smell," I joked.

"Oh, I give up." Steph slammed the book down on the table.

"Look," said Sophie, standing up and yawning. "I think we ought to forget the whole thing and put it down to Kate falling asleep in the tack room and having a nightmare. I'd much rather talk about something constructive like what everyone wants for Christmas."

"Exactly." Emma dragged a list out of her pocket and read it aloud. "Hamster treats for Mickey, new wheel for Mickey, new velvet browband for Buzby, new hay net for Buzby, new hoofpick – folding type, cactus cloth, reflector armbands, black rubber bands for plaiting, bright red tail bandages—"

"Is that it?" I interrupted. "You haven't forgotten anything?"

"I just thought I'd give you plenty of ideas." Emma grinned, unperturbed.

"I've done a list . . ." Rachel hesitated, glancing round. "Well, we agreed, didn't we? At the last Six Pack meeting?" Rachel was the quiet, shy one out of the six of us, so never got teased. She had asked for a Pocket Pony, a dandy brush and pony fiction.

I knew what I wanted for Christmas more than anything and that was a red rosette.

"Ahem." I felt the envelope lying flat in my jodhpur pocket. "There's something I want to bring up for discussion." I paused, waiting for everyone's attention. "It's hot off the press today – nobody else at the school knows apart from Guy and Sandra."

"Well, come on, get to the point." Emma fidgeted, chewing a fingernail.

I pulled out the envelope and the pink sheet of paper inside. "It's a dressage to music competition to be held here on Christmas Eve and it's organized by the Sutton Vale Pony Club. Isn't that fantastic?" I could feel my heart thumping.

"Oh, not that lot," Jodie moaned. "They were all really good, with fast ponies."

"It's a brilliant opportunity," I enthused. "Guy said we could hire the ponies for the day and he'd give us a group lesson to learn the test."

"Test?" Steph wrinkled her nose in distaste.

"Dressage?" Emma looked equally doubtful. "Buzby wouldn't know what dressage was if it jumped up and bit him."

"It does sound a bit ambitious, Kate," said

Sophie, hedging. "I mean we're hardly Carl Hesters, are we?"

"I don't suppose he's making a star appearance, is he?" Emma immediately went into dream mode.

"Dressage is a doddle," I pointed out. "You just walk, trot, canter and do a few movements – a piece of cake."

"For some. For others it's a possible nightmare," said Sophie.

"Come on, guys, don't be so negative. It's about time we did some proper riding instead of launching over cross-country jumps hara-kiri style."

Emma's eyes lit up just at the thought.

"We've got to enter," I persisted. "Besides, it'll be a blast doing our own tapes. Come on, Steph, you're the music buff. Just think of it as getting Monty dancing."

"Well . . ." She hesitated.

I decided to act on impulse. "Look, if anyone finds it boring, I swear on the Six Pack badge" – I raised my hand to my chest – "I'll buy them everything on their list for Christmas."

"Deal." Emma stuck out her hand.

"I'm in," said Steph.

"Me too," added Sophie.

"You're a sucker, Kate. Just wait till Christmas

Day when you've got no money." Steph smiled gleefully.

But I wasn't bothered. I turned away, trying desperately to hide a smirk. This was my chance to shine, to come first. Whereas jumping terrified me to death, I loved dressage more than anything else in the world. And for once I could win.

"Hey, I don't want to break up the party," said Sophie, pointing at her watch, "but the ride leaves in ten minutes and we haven't even tacked up yet."

"Holy Moses." Emma dived for the door. "Let's get cracking."

"Emma, do you have to ride Buzby so close?" Sophie slowed up Rocket who was swishing his tail dangerously.

"It's not my fault Buzby won't stop." Emma rounded a corner of the wood, totally out of control.

"Well try using the reins. That's what they're there for in case you hadn't realized." Rocket lashed out with one of his hind legs and clipped Buzby on the nose.

"Now look what you've done." Emma jumped off, panic-stricken, dabbing at Buzby's nose with a tissue. The rest of the ride, cantering behind, came to an abrupt halt and half the riders either

15

lost their stirrups or collapsed up their horse's necks.

"What's going on?" Guy rode up on his seventeen-hand showjumper which was schooled to perfection.

"Nothing. Everything's fine." Emma hopped back on Buzby who was chewing a branch.

The two o'clock Saturday ride was always packed and usually chaotic when the horses started to canter. As with most riding schools, the horses knew exactly when they were going to go, and set off whether their riders wanted to or not. Some of the more confident riders kicked on too fast and then couldn't stop, and everyone usually ended up in a complete tangle.

"Single file, a horse's length apart please." Guy walked back to the front.

"Can't he go any faster?" A woman behind me, riding Ebony Jane, was driving me nuts. Every time we came to a wider track she kept trying to overtake. Ebony Jane was blowing hard and getting more and more agitated as the woman jabbed her in the mouth whenever we pulled up. Poor Ebby. She was an ancient ex-racehorse with arthritis. She shouldn't really be on this ride at all but Sandra had overbooked so they were short of horses.

Archie skewed to one side as Ebby's shoulder

drew level. "It's single file," I shouted. The woman glowered but drew back, muttering under her breath.

Archie leapt forward as we picked our way along a mossy bank and then dropped down to a pine track where we always cantered. It was a fresh frosty day with a clear sky and the kind of temperature which makes your cheeks tingle. Archie strode out, keeping a perfect rhythm.

The ride began to canter. I broke into a grin and pushed Archie forward. This is what made long boring days at school bearable. As if reading my thoughts, Archie gave a half buck and surged forward.

It was at the next corner, between two oak trees, that disaster struck. I could hear Ebby thundering up close.

"Out of the way!" the woman yelled briskly, cannoning off Archie, hammering at Ebby's sides with her heels, her jaw set and her eyes glazed with the thrill.

For a split second I caught a glimpse of Ben, Guy's showjumper, suddenly launching up, scrabbling, clearing something high in front. Archie rammed on his brakes and ducked his head down. Horses piled up, banging into each other. Rusty, the smallest, squealed out in panic.

"Slow down!" I screamed at the woman on

Ebby, but it was too late. With a sickening crash Ebby fell onto her side.

Stunned and horrified, all I could see was Ebby's brown body squirming to get up, and the awful woman, thrown to one side, howling as if none of it was her fault. Sophie leapt off Rocket, thrusting the reins at Jodie, and ran across. Through the blur of horses in front, I could just make out Guy on foot, running to help.

Ebby still wasn't up. Everybody was very quiet. It had to be something serious.

"This wasn't my fault," the woman shouted at Guy, who asked her to be quiet.

"Come on, Ebby, what's the matter?" I whispered under my breath, straining to see what was happening. Rachel had a hand over her eyes, unable to look.

"It's all right," Sophie's voice rung out. "She's got her rein caught up in her shoe."

Pushing forward I saw Guy wrestling to undo the billet on the bit. Suddenly freed, Ebby scrabbled to her feet, shaking her head, steam rising from her back.

Making a clearing, Guy revealed what had actually caused the commotion. Across the track, completely blocking it, was a barricade well over a metre high. Solid and imposing, it was made from all sorts of rubbish – wooden pallets, broken chairs, an old table, some oil drums and a broken gate. Someone had gone to an awful lot of trouble to build it. Fixed in the middle was a scruffy board daubed with black paint which read: "Keep Out."

"It's crazy." Emma stared at the barricade. "This is a public bridleway."

Right on cue, a man appeared, pushing through the undergrowth with a chocolate-coloured Labrador running at his side. Guy was fighting to get back over the barricade to Ben whom he'd left tied to a branch. Poor Ben. He'd been so brave to jump. If he hadn't, he would have run straight into it. There'd been no time to stop.

"This is private property." The man clipped a lead on the dog and stood glaring at Guy's back, demanding his attention.

"I beg your pardon?" Guy slowly turned round, hardly able to believe his ears.

"You heard me. You're trespassing."

Time seemed to stand still. Guy's face was rigid. "I presume you're responsible for this ridiculous barrier. Have you any idea how dangerous . . ." His voice broke, anger rising up and colouring his face.

I swallowed hard, twisting my fingers in Archie's mane. Rachel caught my eye, her face ashen.

"If you think this is a bridleway, you're

mistaken. It's no such thing. It's private property and I intend to keep it that way." He was tall, slim, with a narrow face and a look of distaste as he kept glancing at the dozen or so horses piled up on the narrow track.

"Horses have been coming down here longer than anyone can remember," said Guy. He seemed to have won back some self-control, although his voice was strangely taut. "There's no way you can stop them."

"Then I suggest you research your facts, Mr . . . er . . . whoever you are, because I assure you, I can and I will. I suppose you're the riff-raff from Brook House, are you? I've heard all about your reputation."

Guy opened and shut his mouth in amazement at the man's sheer venom, not to mention nerve. I could feel my own blood starting to boil.

"Just for the record," said the man, his voice rising imperiously, "I'm Mr Peter Scott, from the Grove Nursing Home. If you want to take this matter further, then I'll see you in court."

I jumped at the name, startled.

"Good day." He turned abruptly and pushed his way back through the path he'd made for himself, dragging the dog behind him.

Everyone was shocked, motionless, trying to

make sense of it all. It was madness. What harm were we doing?

"I'll ride Ben back round by the road," said Guy, sounding cold and horribly furious. "Sophie, you lead the ride home. Just walk. Ask Sandra to check over Ebby. She's still very shaken."

We shuffled round and edged back up the track in total silence. I was only aware of my own breathing and my brain whirring. The four adults on the ride drew together, talking amongst themselves in muffled voices.

Emma trotted up level with Archie. "Have you realized what this means?" she hissed, her round face puffed out with the drama.

Anyone who knew the rides at Brook House knew what Emma meant. Without the track through the wood the only route to the best rides was along a busy road. And the beautiful scenic rides were the ones that most of the adults paid to go on. Mr Scott was going to cripple Brook House, although he obviously didn't realize it.

I groaned inwardly. Just when I wanted to think about nothing but the Christmas Eve competition this had to happen. It was all the ghost's fault, bringing bad luck on the stables. I drew in my breath sharply. Why had I suddenly thought of that?

21

"This is really serious," said Sophie, her face clouded with worry. "It could spoil everything."

At that precise moment I was convinced things couldn't get much worse. Only I was wrong. Dreadfully wrong. As it turned out, this was just the beginning.

Chapter Three

Sophie called a Six Pack meeting straight away.

We were all wound up, still hardly able to take it in. Emma was already composing a letter to send to *In the Saddle* about the importance and preservation of our bridleways.

"What chance do riders have if they can't get off the roads?" Jodie was on her soapbox. "Horses are a part of the countryside, they shouldn't be squeezed out. It's not fair. They've been here the longest."

We sprawled in the saloon, pulling off boots and coats.

"I don't see what we can do that the adults can't," said Rachel, earning a scornful look from Jodie.

"Well we can't sit back and do nothing. We made a pledge, remember? To ensure the welfare of the horses and ponies. If the riding school loses customers then some of the ponies may be sold. It could be Rusty, Buzby, Archie. Who knows?"

Rachel and Emma suddenly looked very sick. I

knew how they felt. I couldn't bear the thought of losing Archie. I'd never be able to go near a riding school again. It would break my heart.

"OK, so what do we do?" Rachel looked round earnestly, trying to hide her panic.

Rachel was a good rider even though she hadn't been coming to Brook House for very long. She was nervous at first and her asthma didn't help but she fell in love with Rusty, the stable's oldest pony, and instinctively he'd looked after her. In return, Rachel wouldn't ride any other pony. Just like the rest of us. We all had our favourites. Luckily for Steph her parents had bought her Monty, but Rachel and Emma were in the same boat as me – relying totally on working at the riding school to earn rides.

"Well, there's no need to look into the legal system," Jodie pointed out. "It'll take for ever and the adults will be sorting that out."

"It seems to me," said Sophie, thinking aloud, "that this Peter Scott needs to know what trouble he's causing. At the moment I don't think he's got any idea."

"Yeah right, and he's just going to welcome us with open arms when we knock on the door."

Sophie told Steph off for being so negative but of course what she'd said was absolutely true.

"There is a way," I ventured tentatively, catching

24

everyone's attention. My heart missed a beat as they all listened expectantly. I'd been formulating my plan all the way home, saving it for the right moment. "I've been to Grove House Nursing Home before." I watched the surprise register in Jodie's eyes. "My grandad, Charlie, lives there and I've agreed to go carol singing on Monday night. Of course if you were all to join me, we could try to get the residents on our side and then approach Mr Scott. He'd have to listen to us."

A bright broad smile broke across Sophie's face. "Kate, you're a genius. That's perfect."

I grinned back triumphantly and turned to catch Jodie forcing herself to do the same.

"We could make our own posters," Rachel suggested. "I've just got some new felt tips."

"Not more carol singing," Steph groaned. "I get enough of that in the school band."

"Will we have to sing 'The First Noel'?" Emma piped up. "Because if we do I'll have to mime the whole lot."

"Enter at working trot and proceed down the centre line without halting. Track left." Guy read out the dressage test.

"If it gets any colder my eyelashes will go numb," Emma grumbled, wrapping her scarf round her riding hat.

"What was that, Emma?"

"I was just saying it sounds riveting."

"OK, who's going to be first?" Guy glanced down the line of ponies.

Sunday morning had dawned arctic cold with a frost like a blanket of snow. My toes had frozen solid from the moment I'd poked them out of bed.

We were allowed on the eleven o'clock lesson because it was half full and Guy was going to run through the test.

The first rider to volunteer was a livery owner on her own chestnut pony who thought she was the riding school's answer to Mary King.

"She's won trophies the size of fridges," Emma whispered, awestruck.

The girl on the chestnut pony flew down the centre line and then proceeded to do the rest of the test at a flat-out gallop. Guy groaned.

"Has anybody got the slightest idea what they're supposed to be achieving?"

Rachel stuck up her hand. "Straightness, rhythm and suppleness through the corner."

Guy started to look human again. "Thank you, Rachel. Now the trick is to look straight at point C and ride forward holding the horse steady with both legs. Jodie, perhaps you could give us a demonstration?"

Minstrel put in a huge buck and then did an

26

extravagant trot up the centre line which Jodie controlled amazingly well.

"Excellent." Guy smiled.

"Teacher's pet," Emma taunted.

Rachel and Sophie did good movements, keeping at the right pace. Emma wobbled and Steph turned right instead of left.

"When you're ready, Kate." Guy stepped out of the way as I pushed Archie forward. I nudged him with my outside leg to wake him up and then broke into trot. Riding up the centre line was always really difficult because horses felt lost without the fence to cling on to. Fixing my eye on point C, I turned and rode purposefully forward.

"You were too tense," Guy said afterwards. "You let him drift to the left and you had no right rein contact. Plus your corner was too wide."

Guy had never criticized me so much before. And he carried on right through the lesson. It was as if I couldn't do anything right.

"Remember to hand your tapes in on the morning of the competition," Guy finished off. "And for heaven's sake, keep it simple. Horses can't trot to rock and roll. Not unless they're exceptionally clever."

"I'm exhausted," said Rachel, collapsing into a chair in the saloon half an hour later.

I felt as if my jaw was going to crack from trying

27

to look cheerful when really I wanted to burst into tears.

Emma pulled off her riding boots and everyone groaned at the smell of her socks. She'd worn the same pair for a week just because they had Milton's head on them.

Jodie was looking thoughtful, which I always dreaded. "Kate, I hope you don't mind me saying so, but you were trying too hard in the lesson today. You need to relax. Loosen up," she said.

"Oh, you think so, do you?" My voice had frozen to a whisper. "Well, that's very nice and you'd know best, of course."

"There's no need to be like that." Jodie raised her voice so everyone could hear. "I was just trying to help."

"Well don't," I snapped. "You might be able to lark around, to 'relax' as you call it, but I'm planning on making it my career, and I bet Carl Hester never relaxed for one minute, or Joanna Jackson for that matter."

Jodie, as thick-skinned as ever, broke into an electric smile. "Well congratulations, Kate, I had no idea. Hey girls, Kate wants to be a professional dressage rider."

I should have known better than to tell everyone my plans. Emma started asking for my autograph so she'd have it when I was famous and Steph

28

started calling me "Goodwood Kate" and trying to get me to do her tape for the competition.

At least tomorrow night they wouldn't be making fun. Grandad used to be in the mounted police force and had seen Sefton, the great police horse who was blinded in the Hyde Park bombing. Grandad had told me all about life with the horses; the training, their unbelievable courage, his first football match and controlling riots. The Six Pack were going to be bowled over. I smiled at the prospect.

The bus was late the next morning, and it was gone half past nine as I turned up the drive to Brook House. I idly wondered if anyone had done my share of the mucking out. It was still biting cold and I noticed the ponies were out in the field wearing their rugs. Archie was playing tag with Buzby who seemed to be winning. As they snorted and cavorted my heart suddenly flipped over as I caught sight of a grey pony on its own in the next door paddock. It was trotting up and down neighing to the other ponies. No wonder they were all prancing around. It looked about 14.2 hands and carried its tail right over its back.

This must be it. The new pony! Guy had been talking for ages about getting another 14.2-hand pony for the riding school. I was buzzing with excitement. Maybe he'd let me be the first to ride it. That would really be something. It looked as if it was a part-bred Arab.

Running so fast my arms nearly overtook my legs, I dived into the office, banging the door back against the filing cabinet. Guy was studying the diary. "Kate, nice of you to make such a grand entrance."

"Oh, sorry." I caught hold of the door to steady myself. "I've just seen the new pony," I gasped. "He's gorgeous! Can I be the first to ride him? Please, please say yes. I'll be really careful. Somebody ought to try him before he's put in the riding school."

Guy stared, blank-faced. "Kate what are you talking about? What new pony? There is no new pony."

"Of course there is. The grey one in the small field, by itself . . ." My voice tailed off. Guy continued to stare.

"I think you'd better show me." He levered himself up and followed me to the field gate.

It was my turn to stare now. I was slowly filled with horror. There was no grey pony. Archie was grazing next to Buzby, peaceful, tranquil, no sign of being excited. Nothing out of the ordinary.

"That imagination of yours is working overtime." Guy shrugged and headed back to the office.

I stayed put, not moving, scouring the fields and the wood for the slightest movement. Something to say I wasn't going crazy. But there was nothing. My chest heaved, my legs felt like rubber. Dizzy with confusion I walked back to the stables. Sophie and Rachel were barrowing muck out of Archie's stable.

"Hey, what happened to you? We've got landed with your chores."

I didn't answer. Words were stuck in my throat.

"Are you all right?" Sophie touched my shoulder, concern traced all over her face. I was leaning against the stable wall. "Only you look as if you've seen a ghost. Oh my God!" Her hand flew up to her mouth. "You have, haven't you?"

Chapter Four

"The thing is," said Jodie, twiddling with her blond hair, wrapping it round and round her finger, "it wouldn't be the first time that you've elaborated on the truth."

Sophie and Steph shuffled uneasily, glancing furtively at their feet. Emma sat kicking one heel of her boots against the other, not wanting to be involved. Rachel was going to be late so there were just the five of us.

"Well you can't blame us for wondering." Jodie tried to justify herself. "You're the only one who's seen the ghost and this mystery grey pony. It's odd that nobody else saw it. For instance, it was me who put Archie and Buzby out in the field and there was no sign of anything then."

"So you're saying I'm lying."

"No, not at all. We're not accusing you," said Sophie hastily. "But perhaps if it were a hoax, now might be a good time to own up."

I felt as if someone had punched me in the stomach. When Jodie had first arrived at Brook

House I'd been caught lying, living in a fantasy world. I used to boast about an uncle in Hong Kong who owned racehorses and was buying me an Arab pony, and a relative in Cornwall who ran a farm. It spiced up my ordinary life and gave me something to talk about. I lived the dream to such an extent I almost believed it was true. But that was then and I hadn't done it since. I couldn't believe that my so-called friends thought I was lying again. I thought we knew each other better than that.

"Well I'm sorry to disappoint you, but it's true, all of it."

"Right. We had to ask," said Jodie, actually looking embarrassed which was a first. Sophie glowed with relief.

"I've seen it!" Rachel shuddered, wrapping her arms tightly round her shoulders.

"You look terrible," said Sandra. We were standing in Ebony's stable helping Sandra poultice one of the mare's forelegs which had blown up with an infection. Sandra's face turned white.

"I think I need to sit down." Rachel's voice came out high and shaky. She looked absolutely petrified. A sudden coldness washed over me. "It was awful," she said, bursting into tears, her small thin face drowned out by her huge terror-filled eyes. "It

33

was just standing there, staring at me from amongst the trees. I . . . I screamed, and it just smiled. A really mean, nasty smile" Rachel trembled and started wheezing.

"Just take some deep breaths." Sophie gripped her hand, trying to soothe her.

"It's all right, Rachel, nobody's going to hurt you," I said warmly. Rachel was a really nice girl. I hated to see her in this state. Besides, it reminded me of the mind-numbing fear I'd felt when I'd been left alone – I could still smell the cigar smoke if I closed my eyes.

Rachel groped in her pocket for her inhaler. Any kind of stress always brought on an attack.

"It's all right, I'm OK." She drew in a long deep breath and exhaled through her mouth. "I'd just put Rusty in the field. I wasn't really paying much attention – you know, thinking about Christmas shopping and stuff. Anyway, I glanced round, and there he was. Peering at me, not moving at all. I couldn't see his face because he had a big hat pulled down low. I remember he was wearing a long coat and he was holding the grey horse, the one Kate had described. The horse neighed at Rusty and pawed the ground but the man didn't move – just stared and then gave that awful smile." Tears sprang into her eyes as she relived the moment. "It was the most frightening thing that's ever happened to me."

Nobody spoke for a long time. Everybody was trying to digest the new turn of events. Something sinister had taken place and we were all touched by it. There was nothing good about this ghost. It meant harm. Real harm. An icy shudder crept up my back.

"I don't think I can cope with this," Sandra mumbled, tearing strips of gamgee off the poultice she was still holding. "I thought we'd got rid of it."

"What?" Jodie suddenly stared at Sandra.

My heart leapt beneath my ribcage. Something clicked in my head, making sense of it. "Sandra, you know something, don't you? You've seen it."

"Yes, no, I don't know." She crossed her arms tightly, uncertainty flickering across her face. "Don't say anything to Guy, or to any of the other riders." She hovered, unsure whether to carry on. "We've got to keep it a secret. Last time it nearly closed the riding school. People were cancelling in droves."

"Sandra, you've got to tell us what's going on." Sophie spoke for all of us.

"OK, I'll tell you what I know, but you've got to promise not to tell anyone, not a soul." Her voice sounded high and unnatural.

35

We all nodded, riveted, totally fixed on what she was about to say.

"Years ago there used to be a manor house here, behind the stables. It got burnt down sometime in the 1800s. Anyway, there was a family who lived here called the Godfreys. They had three children. One day the wife took the two oldest children by stagecoach to London to visit relatives. It was quite dangerous in those days – you'll have done all this in history. Anyway they were murdered, their throats slit by highwaymen. The husband never got over it."

We all drew in our breaths.

"He doted on his youngest daughter, practically kept her a prisoner in house. The only time she was allowed out was to go riding. This Godfrey chap loved horses, spent a fortune on them. A few months after the murder, his daughter, Augustine, went hunting while he was away on business and fell badly at a hedge. She was riding side-saddle and came down with the horse. She was crushed and died instantly. The old man went out of his mind. He took a shot gun to Augustine's pony and had it buried in the garden. The gravestone's still there in the orchard. Then he found out that she'd actually been riding his hunter and he shot that too. Completely demented, he poured paraffin all around the house and stables and locked himself in the cellar. They didn't find his body. Apparently he was burnt to death, along with the house. The stables survived but every so often Godfrey's ghost returns and tries to destroy the stables. People have seen him and this grey horse which was Augustine's pony. Last time he appeared I saw him crossing into the tack room carrying a paraffin lamp. It nearly gave me a breakdown."

It was incredible. Absolutely amazing. Sandra had transported us back in time. I could practically see the manor house, hear the bustle, the servants, Augustine trotting down the steps in her riding habit. It was all so glamorous. But tragic, oh so tragic.

"How do you know all this?" Jodie was the first to recover from the spell.

"Mrs Brentford told me after things started going missing. I was just a young girl then, working for rides like you. After I'd seen the ghost, Mr Godfrey, she took me to one side and explained. She'd seen the whole story in the local paper that day and wanted to tell me herself. After that the riding school was deserted. Nobody came."

We all knew Mrs Brentford. She'd lived in the cottage at the riding school but now spent most of her time with her sister in Dorset. Sophie's dad had bought a half share in the school and Guy had recently taken over as manager and was renting the cottage.

"When you say things went missing, what else happened?" Sophie asked.

"Oh, stuff moved around, someone heard hoofs clattering when there were no horses about. Stuff like that."

"Did anyone smell cigar smoke?"

Sandra looked at me oddly. "How did you know – oh" – realization hit her – "you never said."

"What else?" Jodie asked.

"Bad luck really. One horse broke a leg and had to be put down. He was Mrs Brentford's favourite. There was an outbreak of ringworm in the yard. It was one thing after another."

I thought of the dispute over the bridleway and Ebony Jane falling. It looked like it had already started.

"How did you get rid of him?" Rachel asked, some colour seeping back into her cheeks.

"Don't know really. Mrs Brentford lost her temper and went shouting through all the stables telling him to go away. I think she got a priest to do an exorcism as a last resort. But I think he just went of his own accord in the end." Sandra shuddered.

"What do you think he's planning now?" Emma whispered.

Real fear showed on Sandra's face. "Oh nothing," she said, backtracking, obviously realizing she'd said too much. "It's all hearsay. Don't you kids go having nightmares on me. There probably isn't a ghost at all. Just silly superstition. Forget I said anything."

But nobody was convinced. The ghost had come back for a reason. To do the one thing he had failed to do first time round. To destroy the stables.

"It's got to be here somewhere." Steph marched into a clump of nettles and winced.

"I don't think we should be doing this." Sophie held back. "It looks so suspicious."

The orchard was never used and was just an overgrown mass of gnarled apple trees and towering weeds and nettles. It was like fighting through a wilderness. It was gone three o'clock and we'd finished our chores. The bus wasn't for another half hour. Thick dense fog was starting to settle. It was practically dark already and we didn't have a chance of seeing anything without a torch. Rachel jumped out of her skin when a blackbird squawked, darting low under a branch.

"This is useless," I hissed. "Let's leave it till tomorrow. Ouch!" I suddenly cracked my shin on something hard. Steph leapt through the grass, oblivious to me hopping around in agony. She started scraping the weeds away, scrabbling with her hands.

"What is it?" asked Sophie, peering into the darkness.

"It's the headstone." Emma was craning her neck, hardly able to contain herself. I could see something grey starting to take shape.

"Oh no." Steph squinted and rubbed at the ancient stone. "The writing's worn off."

"No it hasn't, not all of it. Look." Emma came forward, grazing her knuckles as she rubbed furiously at a growth of lichen. I could see the indentations in the stone, a name starting to come through.

"Pagan. Beloved . . ." Emma paused as some of the words were missing, "Augustine Godfrey. Pagan? That's an awful name." She squatted back on her heels.

"What the devil do you think you're doing?" Guy's voice boomed out, incredibly close. Emma keeled over backwards and grabbed my ankle. In the fog and the dim light we could hardly see anything.

"Just looking for some holly," Steph shouted, coming up with a godsend of an excuse.

Squinting, with my hand to my eyes, I could just make out Guy's tall figure coming towards us. "What about the holly bush by the arena, or had you forgotten about that?" He sounded less angry, less panicked.

Steph was frantically trying to kick the grass back up around the headstone.

"It's got no berries," Sophie blurted out, crossing her fingers.

Suddenly an ear-piercing scream cut through the thick air, shutting out all thoughts of Augustine Godfrey. It was a scream laced with pure terror. Another scream. A woman's voice.

"What on earth's going on!" Guy ran down the drive. The fog was so thick we couldn't see anything. More footsteps running from the yard. We heard Sandra's voice, shouting, searching.

"There's someone there!" Sophie pointed frantically as a dark blur came running up the drive. "Crikey, it's Mrs Garret."

Mrs Garret was in her fifties and always came for a weekly lesson and brought enough sugar lumps to keep a sweet factory in production for a year. She was a level-headed woman, and not the type to scream and shout.

"There's a . . . a . . ." She flew into Guy's arms, sobbing and shaking. Guy had to brace himself so as not to be pushed over.

"It's all right, Mrs Garret, just calm down and tell me what's happened, slowly, from the beginning."

Guy's face was white with shock. Whatever Mrs Garret had seen had frightened her senseless.

"Ph-phone the police," she managed to get out. "The police. P-please." A sob caught in her throat. Guy wrapped an arm round her heaving shoulders not knowing what to do for the best.

"What is it, Mrs Garret? What did you see?"

"A man." Her voice came out louder, stronger than before. She fixed her eyes on his face. "He was following me . . . stalking, that's the word. Stalking me, right up to my car."

She drew in her breath. "He just came out of the fog. I ran to my car, but he started walking faster. Then I dropped my keys . . . I really thought . . ." She clamped both hands over her face and stood very still. Then she let them fall slowly away. "That's when I screamed."

"What did he look like, this man?" Guy asked.

"Tall, thin. He was wearing a long black coat. And a hat. I remember the hat because I couldn't see his face."

"I'll go take a look. Sandra, stay with Mrs Garret, will you?"

"What about the police? He's got to be reported. He's a menace to the public." Her voice rose in desperation but at least she wasn't hysterical.

For a brief moment Sandra's eyes caught mine before she led Mrs Garret towards the house. They

42

were strangely blank, expressionless, but I knew what she was thinking. Sophie knew and Emma. And Rachel, Steph and Jodie. You could ring the police, call in Scotland Yard or the army, but how did you track down a man who didn't exist? A ghost from the past with unfinished business.

Chapter Five

"In the bleak midwinter," Emma warbled out of tune. "What comes after that?"

We were all crammed into Mum and Dad's estate car with Mum driving and only one song sheet between us. Jodie said if she'd have had more time she'd have drawn up printouts on her computer.

"It's a carol singalong, not *Stars on Sunday*," Steph said.

I wriggled round, pulling down my new skirt which Mum had eyed dubiously. Outside, fine flakes of snow were falling and vanishing just as quickly. The fog was still thick and if the Six Pack hadn't begged to go, Mum would definitely have changed her mind. She turned left for the Grove Nursing Home.

We all fell silent as the grey gloomy house came into view down a long winding track. Everyone at school said Grove House was haunted but inside it was really bright and friendly. Grandad Charlie had made loads of friends and was always saying there was plenty to do. He looked happier than he ever had when he was living by himself.

Rachel peered up at the grey turrets and the endless blank windows, and shivered. Emma, who would usually have been cracking jokes left, right and centre, kept quiet. Running down the side of the lawn was the wood where, up until two days ago, we had ridden so frequently.

We found Grandad Charlie in the communal lounge glued to *Coronation Street*. Bernie, who had a round tummy and a dodgy hearing aid, was his best friend and had nodded off in the corner.

The night sister came in carrying a tray of steaming mugs and hurriedly arranged us into a little group holding sprigs of holly.

Residents piled in looking vaguely interested. Jodie counted us in to "Away in a Manger". Everyone started at different times and Steph ended up singing something completely different from the rest of us. Grandad Charlie grumbled and demanded "The First Noel" and Bernie twiddled with his hearing aid and then went back to sleep. Irritation prickled under my skin. I'd expected applause, excitement, thanks for our efforts, me being centre of attention as everyone congratulated me on my organizational skills . . .

"Grandad, why don't you tell everyone about the mounted police?" I couldn't wait any longer. I'd planned it all out. How Jodie and Steph would raise their eyebrows in surprise, listening intently. "Grandad used to have a police horse called Paddy," I bragged. "He once had to protect the Prime Minister. And he saw Sefton, the famous police horse who got injured in the Hyde Park bombing."

I couldn't stop the smile of pride curling up the corners of my mouth. All five of my friends were gaping, really impressed.

"Grandad?" I waited expectantly. A warm glow of triumph crept over me. The whole room had gone quiet.

"Well, I think Kate's exaggerating a bit there." Grandad backed off, his eyes suddenly hard. "Anyway it was a long time ago and I don't really want to talk about it." His face shut down with obstinacy and I reeled, stunned, totally thrown.

Grandad loved to talk about his horsy days – he went on for hours, especially with a new audience. I couldn't understand why he was behaving like this. He was making me look a fool – as if I'd made it all up.

"How long have you known Kate then?" He suddenly beamed at the girls. "Has she told you about her ears?" he chuckled.

Horror turned to disbelief. Nobody had mentioned my ears since I was ten. He was deliberately humiliating me, showing me up. I couldn't bear it. Tears burned at the back of my eyes.

"Before we go on with the carols," said Sophie, quickly changing the subject, glancing round the near-full room, "there's something we'd like to talk to you about, something really important."

Steph jumped to attention and quickly passed round the handwritten posters we'd done in felt-tip pen, listing all the reasons why the bridleway had to stay open. "We're sure Mr Scott doesn't realize that without the bridleway the riding school can't function," I said, once Grandad had had a chance to read the poster. "We're hoping that you'll support us and sign a petition."

Just at that moment Mum walked in with a vase of flowers followed by Mr Scott holding the door open.

His face set like stone as soon as he saw the posters. He carefully picked one up, read it, and folded it in half precisely. The atmosphere was heavy with tension. Even old Bernie had woken up and was looking blankly at the telly.

"What is the meaning of this?" Mr Scott's voice was raw with annoyance. Rachel hid behind Emma.

Sophie met his eyes quite steadily. "Mr Scott, we're here to try and convince you that you're making a terrible mistake. About the bridleway that—"

"Stop!" He held up his hand, cutting Sophie off. The room went dead. "You come here, under the guise of singing Christmas carols to the residents, and then blatantly hand round this rubbish." He shook the piece of paper. "Do you know how sick we are of horses galloping flat out down that public path, scaring the residents half to death?"

"I'm sure they didn't mean any harm," said Mum, stepping in. "Kate's very passionate about the riding school!"

"Mrs Richardson, with the best will in the world, I don't think you know enough about the issue to comment."

Mum snapped her mouth shut, firmly put in her place.

"Now, if you'll excuse me, I have work to do." Mr Scott did an abrupt U-turn and left the room.

"Kate! Kate, I want a word with you now – outside." Mum grabbed my elbow and led me towards the door.

"Mum, you're being embarrassing! Mum!" I could have died of humiliation. How could my carefully laid plan crumble into such a disaster?

"Grandad!" I glanced back, looking for support, and wished I hadn't bothered. He was sitting with his head back and his mouth open, blatantly pretending to be asleep.

I glanced in the mirror out of the corner of my eye and smoothed down my thick black hair. Poor boring plain old Kate. I scowled at myself with dislike and picked up my horsy notebook. Maybe I could be a famous equestrian journalist as well as a dressage rider? I could just see people queuing for my autograph. I'd be invited to all the star-studded parties. I could have a column in *Horse and Hound*.

"Kate?" It was Mum's voice again. "Brook House is on telly. It's about the bridleway."

I leapt down the stairs two at a time, crashing into the sitting room, the door banging back against the frame. Ben, my little brother, deliberately started switching channels.

"Hey, squirt, cut it out." I grabbed the remote control and flicked back to the regional news, my heart hammering as the familiar stables came into view.

Mum perched on the arm of the settee. "That's Archie, isn't it? Walking past?"

Sure enough, Sandra was leading Archie and Rocket in from the field, one in each hand. The TV people must have turned up late that afternoon after we'd all gone home. I groaned out loud. A once in a lifetime chance of being on telly and I'd missed it!

"Ssssh." Mum leaned forward and turned up the volume. The reporter's voice boomed round the room.

"*Brook House Riding School has been using the public right of way for the past twenty years as have other riders in the vicinity. Mr Guy Marshall speaking on behalf of the owners of Brook House is shocked by Mr Scott's reaction.*" The camera switched from panoramic to a close-up of Guy, pale and uncomfortable. It didn't sound at all like him.

"*I don't know what all the fuss is about. As far as we're concerned it's a bridleway. There's a sign up saying so. We've done nothing wrong.*"

Mr Scott suddenly came on camera sending a shiver down my back.

"*The issue in question is that it's never been recognized by the council as a bridleway, only by the locals. The signpost was actually made by the local blacksmith eight years ago. Horses galloping out of control are a danger to the residents of the Grove Nursing Home who, quite frankly, have been terrified out of their wits.*"

Someone from the council came on next and said the matter would have to be looked into.

"Red tape!" Mum fumed.

"*In the meantime the police have instructed Mr Scott to dismantle the barricade and are proceeding with prosecution for blocking a right of way.*"

"Yes!" I jumped up, ecstatic. We'd got him!

The camera panned back to Guy. "*Is it true, Mr Marshall, that in recent weeks the stables have been reputed to be haunted, causing a drop off in the number of clients, and that the dispute over the bridleway could be the final straw for the school?*"

Guy looked shocked. "*No comment,*" he eventually forced out.

I sat stunned as the reporter went on to describe Augustine Godfrey and her father's ghost. The picture changed and there was Mrs Garret in her sitting room, talking about the stalker.

I froze rigid, locked in the chair. How could she betray Brook House and go to the press? If the ghost made any more appearances, nobody would go to the riding school. It would be the absolute end.

The telephone trilled noisily from the hall. I picked up the receiver. "Hello?"

"Kate? It's Sophie. Have you just seen the news?" She paused, breathless. "What are we going to do now?"

Chapter Six

Guy was furious. I'd never seen him so bad-tempered. Even the horses looked on edge. Ebony Jane shook her head, snowflakes clinging to her ears and forelock. The outlook was bleak. It looked as if Godfrey's ghost was getting his final wish.

"Christmas decorations!" Emma thumped a tatty box on the saloon table and proceeded to pull out handfuls of tinsel. There were enough decorations in the box to turn the saloon into Santa's grotto.

Rachel pulled a face.

"Look." Emma splayed out her hands in a dramatic gesture. "It's Christmas in a few days time. We can't just sit around thinking it's the end of the world. We've got to think positive. And while we're on the subject," she went on, pulling out a copy of *In the Saddle* and pointing to a recipe for a Christmas pudding for ponies, "I've got all the ingredients in Dad's car. We can do individual puddings for every horse and pony. That should take up most of the morning."

"And it's usually Kate who's the bossy one," Steph grumbled under her breath.

"I heard that."

"Ah, there you are, girls." Guy appeared at the door looking tired out. We knew he was worried about keeping his job, especially as he had two of his own showjumpers to feed and care for. "It's forecast to brighten up this afternoon," he said wearily. "If you tidy up the muck heap you might as well have a ride in the school."

"Cool!" said Emma, grappling with a plastic tree.

I felt a sudden stab of panic. It would be terrible if we had to find a new riding school. Brook House was always so good for rides. Not like some schools where you were expected to work for nothing.

"Well, what are you waiting for?" Emma shot everyone a look, weighed down with purple baubles. "I'm far too busy to help. Besides, there aren't enough pitchforks."

"You turn right at point C," I shouted to Steph who was trying to steer Monty back onto the track.

Sophie was helping Emma with Buzby, the riding school's number one villain. None of us could understand why Emma was so obsessed with him when all he did was buck her off or literally refuse to move.

Jodie led Minstrel into the arena, swirling and cavorting, sending up sprays of sand. The chestnut stallion was brilliant at jumping but became flighty and tense when faced with dressage. Archie might be hairy and stubby, but at least he was sensible most of the time.

"I've just thought of something," said Sophie as she trotted up on Rocket, beaming from ear to ear. She'd just been demonstrating a three-loop serpentine to Rachel. Sophie spent so much time helping other people, she never actually got round to improving her own riding. "Why don't you enter the pairs with Jodie? It's just what Minstrel needs to settle him."

I didn't answer for an uncomfortably long time. My brain was fishing around frantically for an excuse. I couldn't tell the truth – that I didn't want to share the limelight with Jodie. Not after Jodie had spent hours helping me with my showjumping. Guilt made my cheeks prickle with colour.

"Don't bother." Jodie rode across, obviously having overheard. "I can manage on my own, thank you very much."

"Now don't be like that," I said, suddenly finding a voice. "I didn't say I wouldn't."

"Oh please," said Jodie with a grimace. "I've

seen people more enthusiastic about school exams."

"Ssssh," Sophie hissed, cutting in. Guy was walking towards us.

I squinted up at the sky where big heavy grey and white clouds were looming. Even the plastic bags inside my boots weren't keeping my feet warm. Archie snuggled up to Buzby, hoping I wouldn't notice.

"I'm taking Ben and Dillon indoor jumping. Anyone want to come?" Guy's voice was heavy, matching his mood. Everyone yelled yes at the same time. "There's only room for three."

"Count me out!" Jodie backed away, giving me a look which clearly stated she didn't want to be anywhere near me. In the end it was me, Rachel and Sophie.

"Do you think it's safe taking the horsebox out in this weather?" Rachel rode alongside me, peering up at the clouds.

"Of course." I shrugged off her concern. "Guy wouldn't suggest it otherwise. You know how safety conscious he is."

"Mmm." Rachel still couldn't hide her anxiety.

"You worry too much, Rachel," I laughed, throwing back my head, feeling the tiny droplets of sleet sprinkle on my face.

It wasn't far. Just to Horseworld Centre which

55

had a big indoor school and a full course of showjumps including a Road Closed, double gates and a massive wall designed like a house.

Guy always took helpers to put up jumps and replace poles. Last time we came we had to build a grid which was a long line of jumps, all at varying distances. Ben popped through it easily even though one was nearly five foot high.

Rachel sat at one end, Sophie in the middle and me nearest Guy. It was a huge cream horsebox which carried three horses and had a small area for living accommodation. One day I was going to have a similar box with *International Dressage Rider* written down both sides.

We felt the horses shuffle behind as Guy eased carefully round a corner. Rachel had brought a book on the famous Lipizzaner stallions in Vienna and Sophie was asking Guy about dressage.

I was staring out of the window, hoping somebody I knew might drive past. Everybody always looked at horseboxes.

"So does your grandad like Grove House?" Guy asked unexpectedly, throwing me onto the defensive.

"Uh, yes, it's OK. He's got a friend called Bernie who he plays dominoes with. He used to be in the mounted police," I added as an afterthought, then trailed off. "But he doesn't like talking about it now."

Guy eased gently into the first corner of a double bend, dropping gears. He wound down the window to clear some condensation on the windscreen. One of the horses stamped impatiently, thudding against the kicking boards.

Guy went into the second bend, grinding the gears back into third. He was only doing twenty miles an hour. A high stone wall blocked the view of the road ahead. It was only a single lane but nobody ever went too fast. The windscreen wipers sloshed back and forth, dissolving the steady shower of sleet. Guy glanced in the mirror to check he wasn't holding up any drivers.

Rachel was the first to scream out. Ahead of us a black car slammed on its brakes and swerved. "Watch out!" she yelled.

It was going far too fast. Sliding sideways, it hurtled towards the horsebox cab.

"Oh no!" Guy hit the brakes. The headlights from the car dazzled all of us.

"Get over!" Guy hauled at the wheel, shielding his eyes with his arm. The horsebox skidded out of control, hurtling across the road. Rachel screamed.

"Hold on!" Guy yelled, rigid with fear.

I grabbed at Sophie's coat sleeve, sliding down

the seat. Guy's foot was pumping the brake but nothing was happening.

"We're going to die!" Rachel started frantically trying to open the cab door.

"Stop her!" Guy yelled.

"Rachel!" I clawed at her hands, trying to prize them off the handle. "Rachel, don't be so stupid. Sophie, help me!"

Sophie was holding on to the back of the seat, her eyes fixed ahead, locked in shock.

A wild, terrified whinny came through from the back, followed by violent kicking and scrabbling. The horsebox, thrown by the horses' weight, suddenly keeled off in a different direction, helter-skeltering towards the other side of the road.

"Rachel!" I dug my nails fiercely into her hand just as she pulled up the lever. A blast of cold air hit us as the door flew open, crashing against a tree. "Rachel!" The force of the impact tossed her back against me like a rag doll.

The horsebox was skidding helplessly towards a drainage ditch. Rachel started whimpering. The horses, as if sensing imminent danger, flung themselves into a tirade of kicks and squeals, rocking the horsebox even more. With the door ripped open, we could hear every sound.

Everything slipped into slow motion and a kind of weird calm descended. We were going into the ditch. It was inevitable. In a last desperate attempt Guy rammed on the air brakes, but to no avail. Instinctively we all leaned back, sticking our feet out, bracing ourselves.

The front wheels dropped first. It felt as if we were going over a cliff, free falling. Miraculously the box stayed upright. I opened my eyes and dared to breathe. The windscreen was blacked out, rammed up against the bank, clods of soil pressed against the glass. I could hear water trickling. Steam started rising from the engine. A feeling of relief swept through us. But too soon. The horses! There was a mad kicking and thrashing. With a terrible creaking and groaning the unthinkable happened. The horsebox shuddered, and then slowly, as if it wasn't really happening, toppled over onto its side.

Guy howled in pain. I knew something was terribly wrong, even in the pitch blackness. He was caught, tangled up in the steering wheel.

"Guy?" I tried to lever myself up out of the tangle of legs and bodies. Sophie groaned, dazed, her head under my shoulder. "You OK?" I asked, unable to see a thing.

"Yeah, I think so. Rachel?"

There was a silence. "Yeah, I'm all right. What about Guy?"

"Guy?" I could just make out his crumpled body

underneath us. I had my feet lodged against the dashboard and steering wheel to keep my weight off Sophie. Rachel's knees were digging into my back. "Are you hurt?"

His voice was muffled, thick, not his own at all. It was as if he was gathering all his energy together to speak. "I think I've broken my leg. It's caught under the steering wheel." He tried to move and winced in obvious agony.

"Just stay absolutely still," Sophie breathed into the dark, her heart racing.

"You're going to have to climb out of the door above and fetch help," said Guy.

"Maybe someone's there already," Sophie said. "Ringing the police. The driver of that black car must have seen us go off the road."

Relief washed over us.

"Switch off the engine," said Sophie. None of us had registered that it was still going. I could smell the cloying diesel fumes drifting in through the open gap above us.

"The horses," Guy groaned.

My heart almost stopped. The horses. We hadn't thought of them. There was no movement, no noise whatsoever.

"I think they're dead," Rachel said in a matter-of-fact voice.

"We don't know that," Sophie snapped. "They might just be unconscious."

"I can't go up there," Rachel cried out. "I can't see them!"

"Look, we've got to," reasoned Sophie. "They need us, there might be something we can do."

"Don't get near their legs," Guy warned. "Don't get hurt. It's not worth it."

I knew what Guy was trying to say. Horses the size of Ben and Dillon could kill somebody struggling in panic. We had to keep our heads.

"Can you move at all?" Rachel pleaded.

"I'm trapped. It'll probably take the fire brigade to get me out." He bit back a groan and fell silent, gasping for air. "Just get help. Please."

"Put your foot on my shoulder," I told Rachel, and winced as she slipped and her knee dug into my neck. It was lucky that the door had been ripped open in the crash. At least we didn't have to push it open from underneath.

"I've got it." Rachel's head and shoulders disappeared through the gap. I hoisted her up higher.

"Don't fall for heaven's sake," I warned.

She scrabbled out and turned to give me a hand. "No, I can manage. Just climb down carefully." The last thing we needed was someone else with a broken leg. I swung up through the hole easily, school gymnastics paying off.

Outside the road was desolate, bleak, no Florence Nightingale about to offer assistance. The skid marks stood out on the road like a series of burns. Rachel grabbed my arm, speechless. I thought she must have seen the horses and swallowed back fear. None of us had ever seen a dead horse before. I didn't know how we were going to cope. Courage dried up inside me.

Rachel pointed down the road. "He saw me," she gasped. "The black car – it was parked on the verge and when I climbed out it drove away."

Chapter Seven

"They've gone to fetch help, Rachel. It's obvious!"
I had to say that, convince myself. I couldn't start
to think about the weirdness, the cold-heartedness
of being at an accident scene and not helping.

Sophie jumped down behind us. My heart
banged frantically. "I'll look first," I offered.

The horsebox was tilted on its side, the back
end in the air, one of the wheels still turning. There
was no sound. I forced myself to walk round to
the other side. Sophie held back, clutching Rachel's
hand.

It had fallen close to a tree, snapping off a huge
branch which sprawled across the narrow road.
On one side, ripped and frayed, was a huge piece
of canvas which I suddenly realized was the roof
of the horsebox.

I saw Ben's head, poking through a tear,
watching me, absolutely still as if waiting for help.
He snorted and rolled his eyes, almost telling me
to hurry.

"I can see Ben!" I yelled. "Sophie, we've got to get him out!"

"Where's Dillon?" Sophie stared up at the ripped canvas.

"Come on!" I didn't answer. Didn't want to think that far ahead. "We've got to pull back the canvas, make a bigger hole." I started grasping, clutching, tugging at the green cloth in desperation.

"Shouldn't we fetch help?" Rachel said. "I think there's a phone box nearby." She glanced around. It had started snowing.

"OK, you go off and call – we'll stay with the horses. Be as quick as you can," I called after her.

"Whoa boy, steady darling. We'll soon get you out of there." Sophie was with Ben, kneeling down, stroking his huge bay head with a cut over the eye socket, wiping away a smear of blood. "We're going to get you out, yes we are, we are." Tears streaked down her face.

"I need your help, I *can't* do it." I fell back as the canvas loosened, nails showering down on top of me.

"I can see Dillon," Sophie yelled, peering underneath the canvas. "He looks OK. He's even eating his hay."

I felt shaky with relief. It was miraculous that both horses had survived. It never ceased to amaze me just how brave and resilient horses were.

The snow was coming thick now, soft, silent, settling on the grass, the horsebox, the road, our hair.

"The police and an ambulance are on their way." Rachel came back, hugging herself for comfort.

Ben was starting to get restless. Sophie talked to him constantly, smoothing his forelock. We could hear Dillon stamping, agitated, beginning to wonder what was happening to him. I knew every minute counted.

I was overwhelmed with relief as the police and paramedics arrived. The paramedics rushed to help Guy and the police fought to get the horses out. We stood out of the way as they ripped the canvas from the top of the box. The snow was blowing straight into our faces.

Without warning, Ben decided now was the time to escape.

"Stand back! Get back!" a policeman shouted, grabbing Rachel.

Ben floundered, scrabbled, half jumped, half fell through the opening and stood shaking himself, gazing around as if he always got out of horse-boxes this way. He still had his tack on and his rug which hadn't even slipped. Woodshavings clung to his mane and tail but apart from that he was OK. Just a cut over his eye.

"It's a miracle," Rachel gasped, a smile breaking on her face, "He's all right!"

"Dillon!" Suddenly what sounded like an earthquake erupted from inside the horsebox. I could hear legs thrashing, stumbling. Ben whirled round, neck arched, tail raised, neighing to his friend.

"He's out!"

Dillon leaped through the hole, front legs splayed out, reaching out for solid ground. The head collar flopped loose round his neck and the bridle was torn off completely, clanking round his knees.

By now a spare horsebox had arrived and the police rang Sandra at the stables to let her know what was happening and that the horses were on their way. The paramedics had cut Guy out of the cab and we all got into the ambulance with him since the doctors wanted us to be checked out.

Jodie, Emma and Steph rushed to the hospital as soon as they heard the news.

"Guy's going to be OK, but they want to keep him in for observation overnight. He's broken his left leg so he'll be on crutches for a while. He's having it set now," Sophie explained.

Rachel came down a corridor carrying two cups of coffee and insisted I have hers. "He looks

66

dreadful, so be warned," she said as we all made our way to his ward.

"The horses are fine," I told Guy who was propped up in a bed with a mountain of pillows.

"I can't wait to get out of this place," he moaned, even though he didn't look as if he had the strength to cross the room.

"Sophie, tell your dad what's happened straight away. Here's the key to my cottage. Somebody will have to help Sandra do evening stables." His head fell back against the pillows and he half closed his eyes.

"I think Mr Marshall could do with some rest now," the nurse suggested. It must have looked really odd, six girls gathered round the bed. "His mother's due to arrive any minute." Guy groaned out loud.

We were back at the stables doing evening duties. Our parents had agreed to let us move our sleepover to the cottage so that we could help Sandra and keep an eye on the horses.

We had a sleepover once a month taking it in turns in different houses. We had a rule that we only talked about horses or Six Pack business. Last time it had been at Steph's and Emma had to do a forfeit for talking about school.

We were doing everything in pairs in case the

ghost caught us unawares, although after the accident we had other things to think about. Rachel and Emma were the last to finish doing their chores, and emerged from the stables covered in seeds with bits of hay in their hair.

"Right, that's all the horses sorted out for the night," said Sandra. "I'll be in my flat if you need anything." Sandra had a small flat above one of the stable blocks and we could easily phone her if there were any problems.

Chapter Eight

"Steph, cut it out!" The light switch flicked back on, illuminating the kitchen. "This is no time to be playing murder mysteries," Sophie said with a scowl as she ran the kitchen tap.

"I've just put all the sleeping bags in the sitting room," Jodie announced. "And Rachel swears she can get a fire going, although I don't fancy her chances."

"Bacon!" Emma raided the fridge and held up a brown paper bag triumphantly.

"This is brilliant," I exclaimed excitedly. "We've never had a whole house to ourselves before."

"Even if it is haunted," Jodie added darkly.

"I'll help Emma with the butties," I said. "Jodie, you find some firelighters for Rachel, and Sophie, what about plates, knives and forks and things? Steph, we could do with some extra blankets. You could look in the upstairs bedrooms."

"No way," she said, sitting down in an armchair. "I'd rather freeze to death than go up those back stairs."

"Me too," said Jodie with a shudder.

Right on cue, a gust of wind howled under the back door, lifting the carpet. Window frames rattled right through the house. Outside in the glistening blackness, snow swirled around, gathering in depth, banking up in drifts.

I swallowed hard. "On second thoughts, we'll keep to the two rooms. Just to be safe." I bit down on my lip trying not to look anxious. A heavy silence fell over everyone. It was as if we'd suddenly been reminded why we were there.

"I've got it going!" Rachel burst through the door, shattering the stillness. "We've got a real proper fire!"

"We should have marshmallows," Emma said wistfully, staring into the leaping flames. Rachel sat hugging a cushion and the rest of us sprawled out, warming our toes.

"This isn't so bad," said Jodie, beaming as she finished off the last of the Rich Tea biscuits we'd found at the back of a cupboard. "At least we're not cold and hungry, and the horses are safe – that's the main thing."

We'd drawn strands of spaghetti as to who went to check the horses at ten o'clock. In the end it had been me, Sophie and Emma. We'd streaked down the row of stables, flashing the torchlight on each horse, the wind buffeting us, a blizzard working up, driving the snow into a swirling frenzy.

"It's an adventure," Emma had said. None of us had mentioned the ghost. We didn't dare think that we might not be alone.

"Poor Guy," Rachel sighed. "He won't be able to ride for weeks."

All around the cottage there were signs of Guy's presence – showjumping schedules and countless copies of *Horse and Hound*. I knew Guy would be lying in hospital, blaming himself for the accident.

One of Grandad's sayings sprang into my mind. "You can't stop bad things happening. It's what you do when they happen that counts." I clenched my jaw in determination. We were here to protect Brook House. We must not weaken.

Suddenly the telephone rang.

Sophie leapt up to answer it. The ringing went on, loud, persistent. But just as she reached for it, it stopped. "It was probably one of our parents," she said and dialled 1471. "Whoever it was decided not to leave their number."

"Right," Jodie said in a tight voice.

Everyone went very quiet. A small cold dread settled somewhere in the pit of my stomach.

"I think it's time for bed," said Emma, rubbing her eyes.

"Me too." Rachel jumped up, overbright. "Remember, everyone, to leave the lights on."

"Is there really any danger of anyone forgetting?"

"Steph, stop messing about!" I chucked back the duvet in a fit of temper. The darkness clung all around. "Steph!"

Rachel sprang up next to me, cracking her head against Emma's.

"Don't blame me!" Steph's muffled voice came from the furthest sleeping bag. "I haven't touched a thing."

Sophie plodded across to the light switch in her pyjamas. I was still trying to adjust to the blackness, rubbing at my eyes. We'd taken it in turns to stay awake and keep watch but in the end we'd all fallen asleep together.

I could hear the switch clicking back and forth furiously. "Oh no!" groaned Sophie. "The lights are out."

A current of panic coursed through me. The wind seemed to have turned into a hurricane. A terrifying surge burst over the house, rattling the doors, shaking the sideboards and ornaments.

Emma stumbled out of her sleeping bag and knocked over the lamp, sending it sprawling to the floor.

"Where's the torch?" Jodie's voice trembled with fear.

"It's here. I've found it." I grabbed the handle, shaking so much I could hardly turn it on. Then the pale light shone out in front of me. "Jodie? Rachel?" They looked rigid with terror.

Glass shattering behind us made everyone scream. The curtains billowed out, the raw rush of wind howling through.

"The wind's knocked a pane out." Sophie sounded close to losing control. Emma and Rachel clung to each other like lost survivors. Steph put a soothing arm round them, more to comfort herself.

Drawing in a deep breath, I forced myself across the room.

"Kate, be careful," Sophie warned.

The wind blew a spray of snow across the carpet. I could feel glass under my slippers. I don't know what I thought I could do – maybe ram the curtains into the hole, block it up that way. I just knew I had to do something.

The air was biting on my face and neck. My heart was thundering and echoing in my ears. I grabbed the curtains which billowed out against my legs. In that split moment I caught a glimpse of the yard outside.

I wanted to scream but couldn't. It just rose and

fell inside me. I was paralysed. I could barely back away from the window.

"Kate!"

"There's a light on. In the saloon. And I saw a figure. A black figure carrying a can." It was amazing how matter-of-fact I sounded when even my bones were trembling.

Emma started screaming, short gasping shrieks. Jodie clasped the tops of her arms and shook her, ordering her to stop. "We've got to keep our heads."

"I think we'd better phone the police," said Sophie.

"Good idea," Jodie agreed.

But there was no tone.

"That's it. The line's been cut. We're going to be killed, murdered." Emma's eyes rolled in terror. She reminded me of a horse panicking, desperate, out of control. Archie. He was out there. Locked in his stable. Vulnerable. Relying on humans for everything.

"I've got to go." I made a dash for the door. Sophie grabbed me back, her fingers dragging at my arm.

"Are you crazy?"

"Let me go!" I cannoned past, aggressive now, determined.

"Kate! For God's sake!"

I wrenched myself free and whirled to the kitchen door. "I'm not letting him burn the place down. I'm not, I'm not. The horses need us. We can't just leave them out there and we have to warn Sandra. She's in real danger."

They stared at me, their faces empty, stunned.

"I'm coming with you." Jodie pushed forward.

"There's safety in numbers," said Sophie, her face grave. "We'll all go."

Soundlessly we pulled on wellies and Sophie grabbed a walking stick and a cricket bat propped in the hallway. As we stepped outside, the wind grabbed the door, slamming it shut behind us. For a moment I couldn't speak; the wind seemed like a solid force, a sledgehammer. Snow blew into my mouth, numbing my throat.

"Shout, scream, make some noise!" Sophie yelled. "Rachel, Steph, go and wake Sandra."

The light glistened under the saloon doorway. A thought sprang into my mind. Ghosts were spirits – they didn't need lights.

"Get out! Leave us alone!" Emma yelled. Sophie clacked the walking stick on the concrete. Archie and Minstrel whirled to their doors, their piercing neighs swept away in the gale.

I stumbled, nearly falling, and gripped the torch for dear life. Petrol fumes filled my nostrils. Nause-ating. Threatening. Dangerous.

75

Suddenly the door flew open, crashing back against the hinges. A figure came out, hunched, pushing into the wind, running along the side of the stables, escaping.

"It's Godfrey's ghost!" breathed Emma. As he ran, the long cloak caught in the torchlight for a second. It was him.

"There's the horse!" I gasped. Unbelievably, the grey pony I'd seen in the field was tied up at the end of the block, twisting and cavorting on the end of its rope, frightened to death.

Grabbing the reins and unclipping the lead rope, the figure vaulted onto its back, hesitated for one moment, then kicked and clattered away, behind the barn.

My breath locked in my throat. We were all rigid with shock. Then, in the torchlight I saw something blowing about. It was a hat. Sophie ran foward and scooped it up.

There in the dim yellow light, clasping the wet heavy felt, we saw a white label on the inside rim, fluttering helplessly. House of Fraser. Pure Wool. We didn't speak. Just tried to digest the new knowledge. There was no ghost. Just someone pretending. Re-enacting the past for some sinister purpose. Someone real and living was trying to destroy the stables. And this was far, far worse. This was attempted arson.

"I'm going to follow him." I was furious now. Any fear had dissolved in a wave of outrage. I could follow the hoof prints and track him down. They'd show up in the snow – at least for a short while.

"Kate, come back. At least we've scared him off." Sophie followed me to the tack room. "Don't be so stupid. You can't go out in this."

Archie backed away from the door stuffing his nose eagerly in my pocket, anxious to see what I'd brought him. With fingers numb and aching I eased the bit into his mouth. The wind dropped suddenly, a quiet calm descending.

"Kate, why do you have to be pigheaded?" said Sophie as she went to get Rocket's tack.

Ten minutes later, Rocket, Minstrel and Archie plodded silently out of the yard, ears pricked, tails held high, taut with excitement. I gripped the torch, stuffing both reins in my right hand, although a full moon reflecting off the snow produced its own natural eerie light. The hoof prints glistened clearly ahead of us.

Emma stayed behind and waited for Steph and Rachel to return with Sandra. She had strict instructions to keep the door locked, no matter what. I pushed Archie on, buzzing with adrenalin as he powered forward, ready for anything.

The hoof prints changed direction, veering off

towards the wood. There were skid marks everywhere. "Come on," I cried, pushing into canter.

"Watch out!" shouted Sophie.

I didn't see the drifts. Archie's front legs sank down into the snow. He floundered, pawing, starting to panic.

"Turn him round!" Jodie yelled.

He was plunging deeper. Fear suddenly unleashed inside me and I kicked out my stirrups ready to get off.

"No." Jodie pushed Minstrel nearer. "Stay on, make him turn, come back this way. Come on, Kate, make him."

Archie lunged forward, deeper into the drift, the snow up to his shoulders. With a superhuman effort I hauled at the reins, wrenching his neck round.

The look in his eyes was of pure terror. I kicked with my inside legs forcing him to move. Scrabbling, paddling, half jumping, he hauled himself out of the drift. I ended up wrapped round his neck, drenched and exhausted but flooded with relief that we were OK. Archie stood trembling, breathing heavily, steam rising from his neck.

"I hope you're satisfied." Jodie was livid. "He could have broken a leg or anything in there." Tears started to flow down my icy cheeks, more as a release than anything else.

"This isn't about the Six Pack or Brook House, this is about Kate being a hero," said Jodie sarcastically. She wheeled Minstrel round, making patterns in the snow. "Well, I'm going back. Come on, Sophie. We'll fetch help as soon as it's light and then the police can deal with it. I must have been crazy to agree to this in the first place."

Minstrel and Rocket turned eagerly back to the stables. Defeated and totally wretched, I let Archie follow. I took one last look back at the wood, but said nothing about what I was beginning to suspect. It could wait. At least until daylight.

Chapter Nine

A shaft of light filtered through the heavy curtains. Emma was asleep next to me, crashed out with her mouth open. Sandra, who had insisted on staying with us at the cottage, was snoring. Gingerly, I pulled my legs up and out of the sleeping bag and crept over to the door. Silence. Nobody stirred.

I reached for the door handle. This was it. I was going against all the Six Pack rules. Striking out on my own. Did I secretly want a chance to shine, to do something special, to be a hero like Jodie said? I clenched my jaw in determination and, ignoring my inner voice, stepped out into the white cold.

Archie accepted the saddle and bridle without much enthusiasm. The air was still and crisp, the snow thicker than last night. I slammed on my riding hat and fought like mad with the buckle. Nervous now, I led Archie out, praying that Buzby wouldn't start banging his door and wake everyone. Yanking down the stirrup, I hopped and swung into the saddle.

"Come on, boy, it's now or never." I headed straight for the bridleway, ploughing forwards, Archie lifting his knees right up to his chest.

I was pretty sure that whoever had broken into the stables last night really believed there was no one staying at the house. I was convinced the electricity and phone lines had come down in the storm. Whether the person in question would have actually set fire to the stables was hard to say. The spilt petrol could have been meant as a final threat. Whoever it was was desperate enough to go to any lengths to get rid of the riding school. But how did they know that Guy wasn't staying at the house?

I kicked Archie into a faster trot. At least through the wood the snow wouldn't be as thick. I let him have his head so he could pick his own line. The ground looked so different; uneven places were covered over in a smooth layer.

I tried to blank out the fear of being caught in a drift again. I knew exactly where I was going. I couldn't weaken now. Archie surged forward. We turned into the wood, moving as one, in tune with each other's thoughts. I was almost fizzing with impatience now. Snow spattered down from branches. We twisted this way and that, nearly managing a canter.

The sudden stop came from nowhere. Archie

slammed on the brakes, skidding to a halt, his hind legs plunging under him.

I groaned in despair. The barricade had only been half dismantled. It was still nearly a metre high. It should have been taken down. The police had said it would be. I could have cried with frustration. On each side the undergrowth was too thick to push through. The only way forward was over. I couldn't jump. I couldn't . . .

Ever since my first riding lesson, I'd been paralysed with fear at the thought of jumping. I'd make up any excuse to get out of it. Jodie had got me going in the summer and I'd done clear-round jumping at a show but that was with other people pushing me, proper poles that fell if you touched them, not a solid, glaring obstacle with snow piled up on the take-off.

I turned Archie round, choked with disappointment. If I went back now I'd look such a fool. They'd vote me out of the Six Pack. I had to follow my hunch, take back something concrete.

My blood turned to water as I wheeled Archie round and headed for the jump. Three strides out I stopped using my legs and we ground to a halt. It was no good. Guy said you had to believe. Throw your heart over and the horse would follow. I couldn't. I just couldn't.

Grandad Charlie's words sprang into my head.

"It's what you do when bad things happen that counts." What would he have done? What did he do when he rode into riots, with men armed with broken bottles and home-made petrol bombs? I closed my eyes and drew up every ounce of courage. Archie could do it. He was a good jumper. I just had to give him confidence that I could do it too.

I allowed myself as long a run up as possible. I sank my fingers into his mane and reassured him with coaxing words. I counted to ten. Then I fixed my eye on the middle of the jump and clamped my legs round Archie's sides.

"Go on, boy. For me. For Brook House. Jump!"

We hurtled forward, accelerating with every stride. Archie's head rose up, his ears pricked. I squeezed my eyes shut, dragging my fingers through his mane. Before I knew what was happening we were rising up from the ground. I leaned forward, felt my chin brush against his mane, felt the power as he thrust off, soaring into the air.

I was smiling, really smiling. It felt fantastic. Like being in a hot-air balloon, like taking Concorde over the Atlantic. Way out over the other side, Archie spreadeagled his forelegs and landed perfectly, sinking down and then springing away. I'd done it. I'd really done it. A huge real jump.

I galloped away on the other side, leaning into

his neck, streamlined, still hardly able to believe it. A warm flood of triumph crept over me. I knew riding would never be the same again. I'd turned a corner.

Archie neighed suddenly, his ears pricked forward. My breath snagged in my throat, confidence running away. Grove House Nursing Home came into sight. I had to be careful. I must not be seen.

Leaning close over Archie's neck, I skirted round a conifer hedge heading straight for the outbuildings. If my hunch was right, if I'd put two and two together and got four . . . I gave Archie his head, slipping the reins through my hands. "Come on, boy, help me."

The snow was untouched, a fresh layer covering any tell-tale tracks. I glanced up at the house, silent and grey in the early morning light. All the curtains were drawn, everyone was dead to the world. An icy shiver ran up my spine. This was madness. I could be seen at any minute.

I started to panic. I had to turn round, go back. I pulled on Archie's left rein. "Archie, come on." But it was too late. He'd stiffened with excitement, breathing in the air, snorting through flared nostrils. I felt a trace of fear. It was as if I wasn't there. He was totally switched off to me on his back. Leaping forward, he fixed his jaw against the bit and burst into trot. We were careering across the main lawn.

"Archie!" I tugged backwards, my chest hammering.

Outside the coach house, Archie slithered to a halt, dancing and fretting on the spot. Then he opened his mouth and let out a neigh, loud and piercing, and I felt as if I was going to curl up and die. Any minute now Peter Scott would come charging out of the house. I held my breath and waited. But instead there was an answering neigh, sharp and excited, from inside the coach house.

I was right. Blimey. I was right. And Archie had known. I leapt off, flinging away the stirrups, and dragged Archie round to a window near a row of dustbins. I quickly wiped snow away from the pane of glass and peered in, balanced on a milk crate. Archie, irritated that he couldn't see, knocked a dustbin over with one of his hoofs. I cringed in horror but the snow dulled the fall and the bin rolled harmlessly away under a rose bush. With thumping heart, I turned back to the window and looked in.

The grey pony was staring back, pulling on a chain anchored to a manger. It was in an old-fashioned stall and, even from this distance, I could see it hadn't been mucked out for weeks. The scraps of straw were sodden through and piled up with droppings. There didn't seem to be any water. Poor, poor pony. Not a phantom horse at all. Just an innocent real pony, neglected and kept in hiding, with hardly any fresh air or daylight.

I was outraged. What did Peter Scott think he was playing at? First the barricade, then re-inventing the ghost story, scaring everyone half to death . . .

I stumbled away from the window. I'd seen something, at the back, in the garage part. I shook my head in disbelief.

I'd seen the car. The car in the accident. The one that had driven off and not fetched help. It had a scuffed wing and a smashed headlight.

I stepped back further, starting to shake. This was terrible. No wonder he'd thought there was no one staying at Brook House. Archie bulldozed forward trying to gawp through the window. I had to get back and tell everybody. "Come on, boy," I whispered hoarsely. "Time to go." But he wouldn't move. Despairingly, I glanced round at the house, amazed that nobody had heard us.

It was just the same. Dead to the world. Except this time I noticed a broken branch tapping at the downstairs patio doors. The glass had shattered, spraying over the stonework. It must have happened in the storm last night. Why hadn't anyone noticed it? Where was everybody?

86

I started to panic. Grandad! Within seconds a whole stream of terrible thoughts rushed through my head. I had to see him. Grandad!

I tied Archie up, and then dashed for the doors. Any fear had dissolved with the sudden urgency. The carpet was wet through inside, the glass crunched under my feet. I hesitated, taking in the ransacked room, papers strewn everywhere, scattered over a large desk, a chair. By the fireplace, a glass lay broken, shards of crystal glinting in the hearth. Somebody had seriously lost their cool.

Hesitantly, I picked up one of the papers fluttering on the arm of a chair. It was a court order, a bill for thousands of pounds from an oil company. Gripped by morbid fascination, I picked up another and another. The bills added up to a fortune.

Suddenly I heard footsteps outside. Somebody was coming – down the hall. I glanced round frantically for somewhere, anywhere to hide. But I couldn't move. I couldn't breathe. I was glued to the spot. The doorknob turned. I could feel the hairs rising on my neck.

Then it burst open. "Grandad!" Relief rushed through me.

"What are you...?" He was standing silhouetted in the doorway, looking as surprised as I was.

Bernie pushed past in a wheelchair looking fully alert and ready for action. "Where is the scoundrel? Come out this minute." When he saw me he looked mildly disappointed. "We thought he'd come back, we thought you were . . ."

"Yes, I know. I thought you were too." My knees started to shake and grinning lopsidedly, I rushed over to Grandad and hugged him until I nearly choked on his aftershave.

"The rat's done a runner. Left early this morning. The police are on their way." Bernie still looked fidgety, gripping a kind of old police truncheon riddled with woodworm.

"Bernie used to be in the police force," Grandad explained, squeezing my shoulder. "We've suspected old Scotty for weeks. Been doing some snooping. Turns out he had an offer from a company for this place but they would only buy if it had more land for a golf course. That was the reason for the fiasco at the riding school. Thought an old ghost story would scare everybody off. When that didn't work he decided to block off the bridleway." Grandad tutted in disgust.

"He must have been desperate." My brain was racing, threading together the pieces.

"I knew something was up when we stopped getting chocolate biscuits," said Bernie, pulling a face.

"So, where is he now?" I said, wondering what would happen to the old people's home and to people like Bernie who had no family – just the friends at the Grove.

"Heading for the Channel Tunnel." Grandad pointed proudly to a copy of the *Telegraph* with ferry times scribbled down next to the crossword. "He couldn't even get that right. Bernie found the vital evidence."

"So you know about the pony?" I burst out.

"What pony?" Grandad looked shocked.

At that moment a police car pulled into the drive and two officers got out. "Follow me," I said, heading for the front door. "And be prepared for the surprise of your life."

The policeman forced the coach house doors open as no one could find the key. I rushed in first and threw my arms round the pony's neck, trying to blot out the stench of urine and the caked, matted mane that hadn't been brushed for weeks. "You poor, poor pony." I said, my eyes filling with tears.

Archie, furious at being left out, broke free and charged round to the front, nearly knocking Grandad flying. "It's love at first sight," I giggled as Archie neighed in his most seductive voice.

After what seemed like ages and endless questions later, I was allowed to ride Archie home and lead the grey mare which the police decided would be best kept at Brook House until they worked out what to do with her.

I'd never felt more important, but somehow it didn't matter as much as I'd thought it would. The main thing was that Peter Scott would be prosecuted and the ghost story laid to rest. Brook House would be saved and return to normal.

I half closed my eyes as Archie plodded through the snow, the grey mare trotting nimbly at his side. My eyelids felt gritty and my bones ached. It dawned on me how tired I was but I forced it back. Somebody had to look after the riding school and do the morning chores and it was down to the Six Pack to help Sandra who was now in sole charge of all the horses and ponies. A surge of energy coursed through me. An hour later, after taking the long route home to avoid the barricade, we turned into Brook House.

The drive was strewn with familiar cars. All the parents of the Six Pack came surging round the corner, Mum in the lead looking white with worry. Rachel, Emma, Jodie, Steph and Sophie followed, their faces erupting with excitement at the sight of the grey mare.

"You better have a very good story, madam." Mum stared up at me, trying to be harsh but really wanting to cry with relief.

I dismounted, my knees buckling as I slid to the ground. Suddenly all eyes were averted as the police car came up behind me with Grandad waving out of the window. "I think I'll let Grandad explain," I said weakly, buffeted by the two ponies who had decided to use me as a leaning post. I smiled and shivered. "It could be a very long story."

Chapter Ten

We called the grey mare Phantom. It was the obvious choice. We put her in the stable next to Archie and then had to move Buzby to the other side because he wouldn't stop kicking his door with jealousy. After some intensive grooming and a good feed she looked a different pony. Emma insisted she was a Connemara although Jodie put her money on a Welsh cross. We measured her and she stood at 14.1 hands without shoes.

Guy came home from hospital on crutches and moaned continually because he couldn't do what he wanted to do around the stables. In the end he spent most of his time in the office booking up lessons. The riding school made front page news in the local evening paper and the publicity meant loads of new people wanted to ride at Brook House. There was a photograph of me riding Archie with the caption, "Brave Heroine Solves Mystery".

I knew the Six Pack were amazed when I refused to have it pinned up in the saloon and even more surprised when I didn't boast about it every five minutes. But the truth was the whole experience had taught me something important. I knew now that you had to be happy with yourself before you could be happy with other people.

"Kate, Kate, will you stop messing with Archie's tail and get a move on." Jodie glanced over the door, a strained expression on her face.

"Hey, it was you who told me off for being uptight, remember?"

"Yeah, sorry." Her face relaxed into a smile. We were doing the pairs together and Jodie suspected Minstrel was going to do his bronco act, despite Archie's calming influence.

Sandra rushed past in a state, complaining that it was Christmas Eve and she hadn't bought Guy a present yet.

"You're not going to believe this." Steph appeared, looking serious.

"What is this? The new meeting place?" I shooed them both out of the stable, not wanting anyone to witness Archie's plaited tail which had gone disastrously wrong and needed unpicking.

"Emma's done Buzby up like a Christmas tree. He's carrying more tinsel than Woolworths." No sooner had she spoken than Emma led out Buzby telling us that all dressage riders walked their horses round before the event to calm them down. If Buzby got any calmer he'd fall asleep.

"I'm surprised you didn't hang baubles from his ears," Steph teased.

The dressage test started in an hour's time with twelve to fifteen in each class and Guy judging. We'd all handed our tapes in and nobody would know what anyone else was playing until the competition. The yard was buzzing with all the regular riders. Archie had been booked for two more tests with another rider but at least I was going first.

"I'm dying with nerves." Sophie came up, pinning her Six Pack badge onto her jacket. "Whose idea was this? Kate!" she groaned. "You promised we'd enjoy this. It's worse than cross-country. Everybody can see your every move. It's like being in a goldfish bowl."

"That's the idea," I laughed. "You're supposed to impress the judge. It wouldn't be much good if he couldn't see you."

"What's this?" Steph swivelled round as a white mini-van came up the drive. The snow had turned into a sludgy mess, piled up at the roadside.

"It's Grandad!" I was ecstatic.

"And all the Grove House residents by the looks of it." Steph narrowed her eyes.

94

"More people to perform in front of," Sophie groaned.

Emma paraded Buzby past the van and then came trotting back with her eyes wide with amazement. "They've got an old lady in there who's a hundred and one," she gasped. "And she thinks dressage is some kind of fashion show. She asked if she might meet Joanna Lumley."

Guy hobbled up on his crutches looking rather subdued. "Kate, there's something I need to tell you." I hovered in front of Archie's tail wondering if they'd changed the test at the last minute. "There's been a mix up with the bookings. Archie's got another rider first. You follow twenty minutes after."

I could feel possessiveness and resentment rising up inside me. The Six Pack watched me as if I was a volcano about to erupt. "I think I'll go for a walk," I said in a tight voice.

"Grandad, it's not fair, I've worked so hard for this." We walked slowly down the drive, Grandad looking really smart in his best suit and overcoat. "I've been schooling Archie for weeks. We'll never win now. He'll anticipate the test. He'll do all the transitions too early."

"But you're still taking part?"

"Oh yes."

95

"Well that's the main thing, surely? Kate, you're thirteen years old. This is your first test. Be satisfied that you've got the chance. If you want to be a professional horsewoman you've got to learn to cope when things go wrong. Because they will do, no matter what you do. Because that's life. And that's what separates the champions from the also-rans."

I drew up short, rocked by his words. I'd expected sympathy. A caring ear. But then things started falling into place. Grandad making fun of me at the home in front of my friends, refusing to talk about his days in the mounted police. He was deliberately taking me down a peg or two. Trying to tell me not to take myself too seriously, not to blow my own trumpet, to realize that actions were far better than words.

"That was fantastic." Rusty scuttled out of the arena with Rachel red-faced but glowing with pleasure. "It all went so fast! I can't believe I remembered everything."

"Tell me I'm seeing things," said Steph, open-mouthed, as Emma ran out of the toilet dressed as Father Christmas.

"Hold Buz, will you? I've got to fix this beard," she said.

The tannoy system crackled into life with "Santa

Claus is Coming to Town". Emma bopped round the arena with Buzby bucking like mad to get rid of his tinsel. The audience, huddled in cars to keep warm, went wild. Everyone agreed that dressage to music was the best thing since showjumping.

Steph did an Elvis Presley medley and Sophie stuck to Robbie Williams who she was openly in love with.

All too quickly it came round to my turn and I was more nervous than I'd ever imagined. Archie pulled a face when he realized he had to go back in and do it all over again. Sophie clutched my arm and jokingly said she was expecting big things. All she did was pile on more pressure. My hands started shaking like leaves. Guy sat in a car at the top end of the arena with a clipboard, writing down marks. My stomach lurched as I rode Archie round the outside track waiting for the car horn to tell me when to start.

K – medium walk. E – turn right. B – track left. I scrambled through the test in my mind.

The horn bleeped and, with my heart hammering in my throat, I swung Archie round onto the centre line. At the same moment Pavarotti wafted out of the loudspeakers. We'd begun. Every stride we took would either win or lose marks.

I tensed my hands on the reins and suddenly remembered I'd forgotten to pin on my Six Pack badge. It wasn't there. On my lapel. Where it should have been. I froze. And then the unthinkable happened. I went blank. I couldn't remember the test. Left or right? Which way? Panicking, I pulled Archie to a halt.

The music cut out. Guy tried to point through the windscreen but my eyes were just a blur. I'd lost everything. Time stood still. I could feel everyone watching, wondering what I was playing at.

Suddenly, ducking his head down, Archie grabbed the bit and dashed forwards, skimming round the right-hand corner. The horn didn't blow to say we'd gone wrong. The music came back on, strong and powerful. Archie was taking me through the test!

It was like magic. I could feel him straining, trying to do everything right. Flex his neck, take long strides, push his hind legs under him. The test came flooding back into my mind. Sitting quietly, taking a deep breath, I started to ride, really ride, putting every ounce of concentration into my position, the movements, keeping straight, putting on a display for everyone to see. I could have been an Olympic rider.

Archie was floating, dancing through the air. I could hear the applause, see the Union Jack flag waving in the stadium. I was on the verge of winning a gold medal. I turned up the centre line and halted in front of the judge, bowing dramatically, one hand moving off the reins down to my side. And then I was back at Brook House. Riding out of the sand arena, my arms slung tightly round Archie's neck.

"Bad luck." Sophie grimaced, almost embarrassed. "It could have happened to anyone."

And then it came back with a dull thud. No matter how well Archie had performed, I'd made an error. Let him down. He'd given me everything and I'd blown it. All the old feelings of dislike came flooding back. I was just plain old boring Kate and yet again I'd stuffed up.

"You'd be better off with somebody else." I glanced away, not wanting Jodie to think I was upset. "Sophie did a really nice test. It's not too late to change the entry."

"No." Jodie carefully did up Minstrel's throat lash not wanting him to pick up her nervousness. The Arab was a live wire at the best of times.

"What do you mean, no?"

"I mean, no. We agreed to do the pairs together and that's exactly what we're going to do."

I sucked in my breath with exasperation. "Why do you always have to be so stubborn? So pig-headed? Don't you understand? I can't go back in that ring!"

Jodie smiled annoyingly. "Exactly. That's why I'm not changing partners."

"You really, really get up my nose. D'you know that?"

Jodie grinned. "Of course. And you get up mine. But that doesn't mean we're not best of friends who help each other. Now pass me that mane comb and stop whingeing."

"Kate! Kate!" Emma ran towards us, her shiny black boots getting splattered with mud as she leapt through a puddle. "You've won! You've won!"

I couldn't be doing with Emma's jokes right now. I was having difficulty enough not bursting into tears, but there didn't seem to be any escape. "Ha, ha very funny," I grumbled, tensing my jaw so it didn't tremble.

"But honestly. Guy's called your number. You've got to collect your rosette. I've come fourth for artistic merit."

"Emma, this isn't very funny. Can't you see Kate's upset?"

"But *honestly*. You don't understand. You only lose two marks for forgetting the test. Kate's romped it."

"If this is a joke, Emma, I shall personally cut all your Christmas presents into shreds and then start on you." Shakily, I followed her to Guy's car.

100

"It's true. It's true. Look."

The scoresheet was stuck onto the back window.

"Now do you believe me?" Emma said.

The rosette was bright red with "Brook House Riding School" printed in the middle. It was much bigger than ordinary rosettes and Archie thought his Christmas had come early and tried to eat it.

The Six Pack totally dominated the places and the younger riders all looked up to us as if we were the England team. All the work over the past year had paid off. We were all becoming good riders.

"I've got to admit, it's an excellent riding school," said a woman standing next to me as she examined my rosette, back and front. "My daughter wants to be a famous dressage rider, you know?"

A smile caught at my lips as my heart gave a little jump. One day. One day.

Jodie and I came second in the pairs. Grandad and everyone else from Grove House left after sherry and mince pies in the saloon. Everyone was celebrating, even though the future of the home was uncertain. Peter Scott had been picked up and charged but there was still so much to untangle. Grandad was bringing Bernie and two others over for Christmas dinner so we'd have a houseful.

101

Guy then surprised us all by making an announcement.

"There's to be a new addition to the riding school," he said, then paused to add to the suspense. "Phantom is now officially a Brook House pony and will be starting to give rides in the new year."

Samantha Alexander
Riding School 5: Sophie

*Six very different girls – Jodie, Emma, Steph, Kate,
Sophie and Rachel – bound together by their passion
for horses.*

*"You just can't help getting involved in my life, can you?" I
could hear my voice rising, cracking with rage. For once
Natalie just stared, speechless. "This was my chance," I
shouted. "They asked me first. Me!"*

Sophie cannot believe her luck when the pony magazine
In the Saddle visits Brook House Riding School. She lands
the star role in a photo story about a horse superstar. But
her sister Natalie is determined to muscle in where she's not
wanted.

A selected list of SAMANTHA ALEXANDER books available from Macmillan

The prices shown below are correct at the time of going to press. However, Macmillan Publishers reserve the right to show new retail prices on covers which may differ from those previously advertised.

RIDING SCHOOL

1.	Jodie	0 330 36836 2	£2.99
2.	Emma	0 330 36837 0	£2.99
3.	Steph	0 330 36838 9	£2.99
4.	Kate	0 330 36839 7	£2.99
5.	Sophie	0 330 36840 0	£2.99
6.	Rachel	0 330 36841 9	£2.99

HOLLYWELL STABLES

1.	Flying Start	0 330 33639 8	£2.99
2.	The Gamble	0 330 33685 1	£2.99
3.	The Chase	0 330 33857 9	£2.99
4.	Fame	0 330 33858 7	£2.99
5.	The Mission	0 330 34199 5	£2.99
6.	Trapped	0 330 34200 2	£2.99
7.	Running Wild	0 330 34201 0	£2.99
8.	Secrets	0 330 34202 9	£2.99

All Macmillan titles can be ordered at your local bookshop or are available by post from:

Book Service by Post
PO Box 29, Douglas, Isle of Man IM99 1BQ

Credit cards accepted. For details:
Telephone: 01624 675137
Fax: 01624 670923
E-mail: bookshop@enterprise.net

Free postage and packing in the UK.
Overseas customers: add £1 per book (paperback)
and £3 per book (hardback)